What Month Is It?

Written by
Sandy Parker

Illustrated by
Cathy Hofher

just think
B O O K S

Special thanks to Sondra Lewis and Linda Hemphill
for sharing your wisdom.

Text copyright © 2004 by Sandy Parker
Illustrations copyright © 2004 by Cathy Hofher

Design by Cathy Hofher

Published in United States of America by:

Just Think Books

Imprint of Canary Connect Publications
605 Holiday Road, Coralville, Iowa 52241-1016

Library of Congress Cataloging-in-Publication Data

Parker, Sandy, 1965–
    What month is it? / written by Sandy Parker ; illustrated by Cathy Hofher.
        p. cm.
    Summary: A young boy's year of traveling to cities in the United States introduces
the months of the year, numbers from one to twelve, and the concept of alliteration.
    ISBN 0–9643462–5–7 (Hardcover : alk. paper)
    [1. Months—Fiction. 2. Counting. 3. Travel—Fiction.] I. Hofher, Cathy, ill.
II. Title.
    PZ7.P2355Wh 2004
    [E] —dc22

                                  2003026798

Audience: Ages 4–9.
Library Reinforced Binding Acid-Free Paper
Printed in the United States of America

www.JustThinkBooks.com

10 9 8 7 6 5 4 3 2 1

To My Family
For Where We've Been,
Where We Are,
and Where We're Going–
Just Imagine!

s.p.

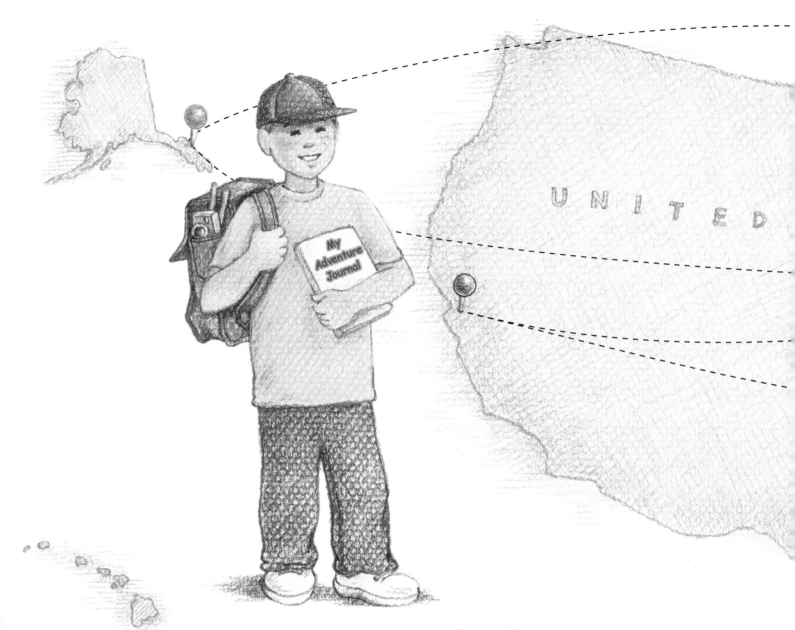

Hi, my name is Sam.
Last year I traveled across
the United States.

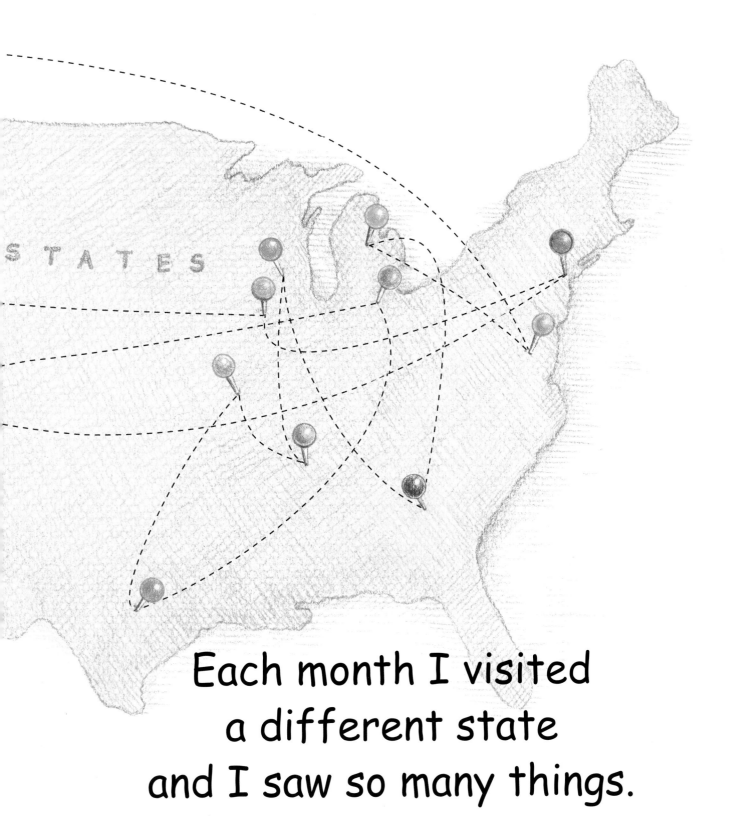

Each month I visited
a different state
and I saw so many things.

In January,
I went to Juneau, Alaska.

I saw 1 silly snowman.
It was the New Year.

In February,
I went to Fairfax, Virginia.

I saw 2 happy hearts.
It was Valentine's Day.

In March,
I went to Midland, Michigan.

I saw 3 swaying swings.
It was windy.

In **April**,
I went to Atlanta, Georgia.

I saw 4 unique umbrellas.
It was rainy.

In **May**,
I went to Madison, Wisconsin.

I saw 5 fancy flowers.
It was sunny.

In June,
I went to Jackson, Tennessee.

I saw 6 big baseballs.
It was fun.

In July,
I went to Jefferson City, Missouri.

I saw 7 funny firecrackers.
It was the 4th of July.

In **August**,
I went to Austin, Texas.

I saw 8 camping cowboys.
It was hot.

In September,
I went to Sylvania, Ohio.

I saw 9 large leaves.
It was autumn.

In **October**,
I went to Oakland, California.

I saw 10 painted pumpkins.
It was Halloween.

In November,
I went to New York, New York.

I saw 11 feasting firefighters.
It was a time to be thankful.

In December,
I went to Davenport, Iowa.

I saw 12 pretty presents.
It was a month to celebrate!

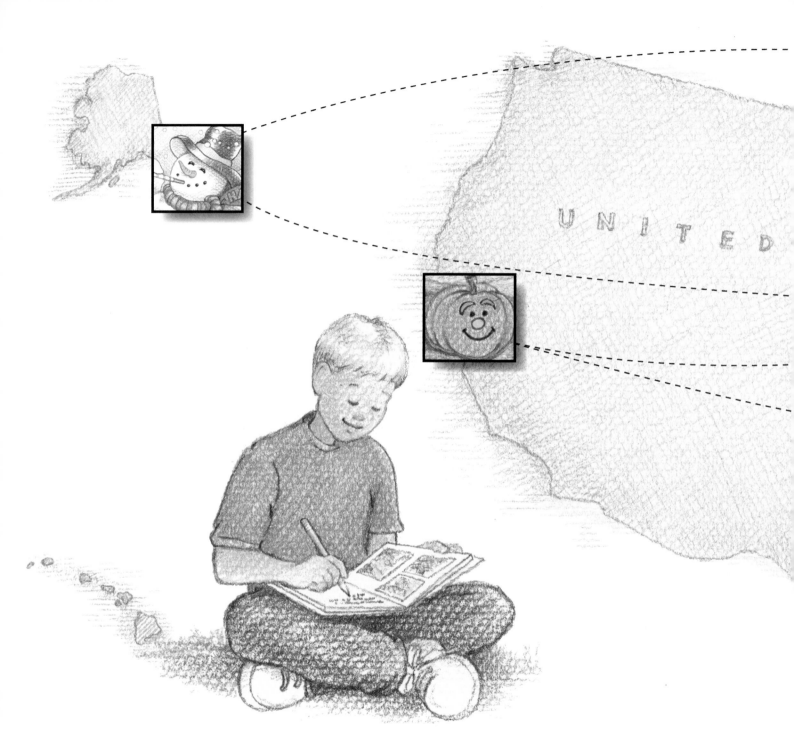

What a wonderful year I had.

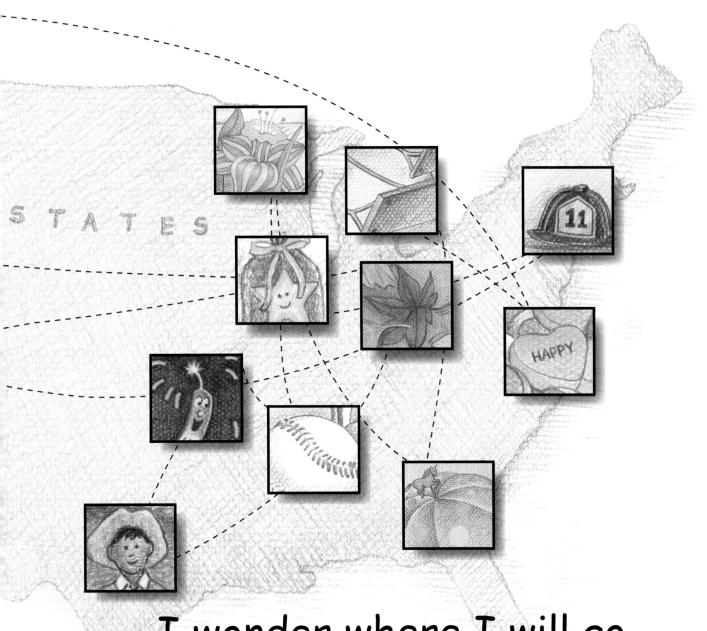

I wonder where I will go
and what I will see next year.
Let's think.

About the Author

Main Street Studio, North Liberty, IA

Sandy Parker enjoys helping children to read and encouraging them to use their imaginations. Utilizing *What Day is Today?* and *What Month Is It?*, she is able to channel her passion by reading and helping with literacy in classrooms throughout the United States.

Sandy and her husband Phil, a football coach, and their two children, Tyler and Paige, currently live in Coralville, Iowa. She is a Michigan native and has also lived in Ohio.

About the Illustrator

Jennifer Donner

Cathy Hofher studied illustration at the Ringling School of Art and has been a professional graphic designer and illustrator for over 20 years. Her love for art and reading guided her toward a career as a children's book illustrator.

The pictures in *What Month Is It?* are rendered in colored pencil. This is Cathy's fifth children's book.

A North Carolina native, Cathy now lives in Williamsville, New York with her husband Jim, a football coach, their three daughters, a cat, and a dog.

In Sandy Parker's first book, ***What Day is Today?***,
children enjoy finding the phonetic objects that correspond
with the first letter of the day (i.e., stones, smile, etc. on Sunday.)

More fun awaits in ***What Month Is It?***
as you discover the phonetic objects that correspond
with what Sam saw (i.e., scarf, stars, skis, stripes, etc. in January.)

Happy Hunting!

Visit www.JustThinkBooks.com
for Curriculum Guides and fun, interactive ideas